# ONE MAN'S WILL

## AN AMISH ROMANCE

Naomi Troyer

# Contents

# Chapter 1
# Covered in Mud

"Don't jump in the puddle...." Faith Glick called out a second too late.

The little boy looked up at her with guilt in his eyes and a smile a mile wide. "I'm sorry, Faith."

Faith laughed and shook her head. "Well, you're already covered in mud. Might as well make the best of it."

Daniel Hauptfleisch didn't need to be told twice. His laughter filled the spring morning even as birds joined in with happy chirps and whistles. Daniel splashed, jumping with both his feet in the puddle, splashing mud onto his clothes and his face.

Every drop of mud would make a memory. Faith tried to convince herself as he soiled his clothes even more. She wouldn't think of the time it would take to wash his clothes, instead, she would focus on what a good time he was having.

"Faith, kumm! Splash with me," Daniel called out, waving his hand at her.

Faith realized that at twenty-one, splashing in the mud with a five-year-old was hardly acceptable, but it was hard to resist Daniel's laughter as he continued to play. Both Daniel's parents worked in town, but he didn't seem to mind, since Faith had been his babysitter ever since his second birthday.

She was a second mother to him, just like he was a little brother to her.

Faith finally gave up on trying to be grown up and lifted her skirt before she jumped into an even bigger puddle. The muddy water splashed all over her dress, splattering mud onto her face, her hair, and, to Daniel's great joy, his face.

"You're not doing it right; you should go like this!" Daniel cried out with glee before stomping his feet in the water, making Faith laugh even more.

From the corner of her eyes, she noticed an Englisch car pull up beside the barn of her home. She didn't give it a second thought, accepting that her parents perhaps had a visitor from town.

"You're not doing it right!" Faith teased and splashed even more.

She saw a man in a suit climb out of the car and approach their porch. From her mother's confused expression on the porch, Faith knew her mother hadn't been expecting the Englischer. Curiosity made her keep glancing over towards her own yard from where she was playing with Daniel in the neighbor's yard.

"Faith, over here."

In the split-second Faith had been focused on what was going on at her home, Daniel had come up with a mischievous plan. She turned, just in time to get splattered with a ball of muddy goo all over her face.

"Daniel!" Faith cried out in shock. "That's not nice. It's in my eyes."

Daniel could be a handful, but he had a sweet heart. He rushed over to her and offered her his handkerchief. "Here you go, sorry."

Faith's heart melted at the shallow tears in his eyes. "It's all right. Why don't we…"

"Faith!" her mother's voice called from the fence.

"Mamm?" Faith called back as she took Daniel's hand and approached the fence. "Jah?"

Her mother glanced at Faith's mud-covered appearance and let out a heavy sigh. "Today of all days…" She shook her head and shrugged. "Well, nothing to be done for it now. I'll get Daniel cleaned up. There's someone waiting to see you in the kitchen."

Faith's brow creased. "The Englischer wants to see me? Why?"

"Don't keep him waiting." Her mother scowled before opening the gate adjoining the yards and taking Daniel's hand from her. "Go on, Faith."

Faith glanced down at her dress and wished she hadn't played in the mud. Her dress was covered with splotches of mud, and her ears itches from the splashes that had reached that high. She quickly crossed the yard, scrubbing her face with the handkerchief, hoping at least her face would be clean when she stepped into the kitchen.

She bounced up the steps and through the front door before making her way to the kitchen. Faith could smell that her mother had just put on a fresh pot of coffee.

"Hullo?" Faith asked as she saw the Englischer sitting at the table with a folder in front of him. "You'll have to excuse my appearance."

His smile was kind as he stood up. "Mr. John Anderson. I take it you're Faith Glick?"

"Jah," Faith nodded. "It's a pleasure to meet you."

Faith couldn't help but hope he'd say what he had to before she dripped mud all over her mother's floor.

"I noticed you playing with the little boy. Looks like you were having fun," Mr. Anderson said, taking a seat and motioning for Faith to do the same.

Faith sat down, hoping that she didn't cover the chair with mud as well. "Jah, I watch Daniel four days a week while his mamm works in town. We have a lot of fun together."

"Your mother mentioned that." Mr. Anderson opened the folder in front of him and cleared his throat. "Did your mother tell you why I am here?"

"Nee, she uh... had to clean Daniel up," Faith explained.

"Right, so I'll start at the beginning. Your grandfather, Levi Stoltzfus, passed away a few days ago. I'm sorry for your loss."

Faith frowned before her eyes widened with recognition. "The one in Lancaster County. I've never met him, but mamm says he was a kind mann."

"Yes, he was. I'm the attorney for his will. It's taken me a couple of days to track you down, but now that I have, I'm happy to inform you that your grandfather left you half of his property and assets... in Lancaster County," Mr. Anderson pointed out as if to make sure Faith understood.

Faith shook her head, the mud and Daniel completely gone from her mind as she searched the man's eyes. "He left me half of his farm? Why would he do that?"

"You're his only grandchild. I'll give you time to let it sink in, but here is my information should you have questions. You'll need to come to Lancaster County as soon as possible to take your half of the ownership." Mr. Anderson passed her the folder along with a business card.

Faith nodded, still in shock. "Denke."

She heard the man leave and, for a moment, just stared at the folder before her. Why would a man she didn't know leave her half of everything he owned?

"Faith, what did he say?" her mother asked, coming into the kitchen with a cleaner Daniel by her side.

"He... uhm... he said that grandfather Stoltzfus passed away," Faith said, shaking her head with confusion.

"Jah, he told me that as well. Why did he need to speak with you?" her mother asked as she offered Daniel an apple to keep him busy.

Faith met her mother's confused expression with one of her own. "Because he left me half his farm and his assets. I need to go to Lancaster County to accept ownership."

Her mother's face eased into a gentle smile. "He bequeathed his estate to you in his will?"

"Half of it," Faith nodded with a shrug. "What am I going to do with half a farm, Mamm?"

"We'll figure that out later, but for now, why don't you wash up? You look like something that was dragged after a buggy." Her mother cocked a brow at the mud drippings on the floor.

Faith cringed. "I'm sorry, I'll be right back."

Faith headed to the wash room but her mind wasn't on the mud at all, instead it was on grandfather she had never met and why he had bequeathed her in his will.

# Chapter 2
# A Puzzling Introduction

Gabriel Lapp had gotten up at dawn to get all the chores done before he needed to go into town. He didn't mind going to town, but he couldn't help but feel a little anxious about the woman he had to collect from the bus stop.

When the lawyer saw him after Levi's funeral, Gabriel had been a little surprised to learn that Levi had left half the farm to family in Ohio. He had always known about Levi's daughter who had moved to Ohio to be married shortly after being baptized, but in the twenty-one years he had lived on Levi's farm, he had never seen her.

Which begged the question, why would Levi give her half of the property if she hadn't even bothered to visit in all these years?

Besides, she would be at least fifty years or older. People didn't really move and resettle at that age, at least not Amish people.

Gabriel couldn't help but feel a little bereft knowing that he had to share his inheritance. Levi had been like a father to him, albeit an older one, but he had been the only father Gabriel had ever known.

This farm, he thought as he glanced over the fields, the only home he'd ever known.

Now suddenly he had to share it with a stranger.

He respected Levi's wishes, but that didn't mean he was happy about it.

The lawyer saw him the day before to inform him that his co-inheritor would arrive in town on a bus this morning. It had been more of a demand than a request that Gabriel collect her from the bus stop and take her to the farm.

Gabriel glanced at the sun and knew he had a little more than an hour before he needed to leave. He still needed to clean the kitchen, wash the floors, and put fresh linens on the spare bed. All chores that wouldn't have been necessary if Levi hadn't left him a surprise in his will.

With a sigh, Gabriel started towards the house, thinking of everything he still needed to do. Farm work, important work, he reminded himself.

The kitchen wasn't dirty, but there were a few dishes in the sink. After Levi's funeral, Gabriel had slacked off with the dishes over the last few days. After pouring the hot water into the basin, he added soap. He placed the dishes and the cups in the sink to allow them to soak while he changed the bedding in the spare bedroom.

Levi had taught him how to make a bed. A fresh sheet, tucked with perfect corners beneath the mattress. Then a second flat sheet, with an embroidered strip at the top which was tucked into the mattress as well. Finally, he opened the linen chest and pulled out a quilt Levi's wife had made years before. He spread it over the bed and fluffed the pillows. Pulling back the curtains and opening the windows allowed the fresh air to dance into the room.

He didn't know what Levi's daughter was like, but she wouldn't be able to accuse him of not being a suitable host. Levi had taught him well and he would make Levi proud, even now that he wasn't there to see it for himself.

Standing back, he assessed the room and decided it would have to do before he quickly fetched a fresh lantern to place on the nightstand.

Once the dishes and the floors were done, Gabriel hitched the horse to the buggy and headed into town. All the way there, he wondered what Levi's daughter would be like. Would she be kind and generous like Levi, or would she be cool and coldhearted and treat him like an intruder?

After all, Levi had been her father, not his.

Gabriel stopped at the bus stop at the exact time the bus pulled in. He climbed out and wondered how he was going to recognize Levi's daughter. Since photos weren't allowed in their culture, he did not know what Levi's daughter looked like.

One by one, people disembarked from the bus. Englischer after Englischer climbed off and collected their luggage before greeting their waiting friends and family. Just when Gabriel was certain that Levi's daughter had decided not to come, a young Amish girl climbed off the bus looking lost.

For a moment, he stood and watched her from a distance. Unlike the Englischers, she thanked the man who helped with her suitcase, before she moved to a bench and sat down. She looked frightened and more than a little intimidated.

Gabriel didn't move.

The girl he was looking at was younger than him, by five years at least. She couldn't possibly be Levi's daughter, he thought to himself as he decided what he was going to do.

Her blonde hair was braided neatly into her prayer kapp, her bright blue eyes darting left and right as if she was waiting for someone. The bus pulled away, eager to reach its next stop, and yet the girl remained on the bench.

Gabriel sucked in a deep breath before he approached her. Her eyes shot up to meet his when he stopped in front of her. "Hullo."

"Hullo," she returned shyly.

"You couldn't possibly be Levi Stoltzfus's dochder, could you?" Gabriel asked.

She shook her head, and Gabriel sighed with relief. His co-inheritor hadn't come, which meant that according to the terms of the will, he would inherit the farm in full.

"I'm his granddaughter. Faith Glick. Are you..." her words trailed off as she reached into her pocket and glanced at a piece of paper. "Gabriel Lapp?"

"Jah?" Gabriel nodded, a little confused.

"Gut, I was afraid you'd forget to come and get me," Faith said with a sigh of relief as she stood up and reached for her suitcase. "Where is the buggy?"

For a moment, Gabriel was completely confused. The lawyer had said something about Levi's daughter, but now that he thought back, he couldn't be sure exactly what had been said. He had been overcome with grief and could only remember snippets of the conversation. "Where's your mamm?"

Faith frowned at him with curiosity in her eyes. "At home... in Ohio. The lawyer said I could come alone."

"On your mother's behalf?" Gabriel asked, even more confused.

"On my own behalf. I'm the co-inheritor of Levi's property and assets," Faith explained.

Levi swallowed past the confusion. "I thought... your mamm... never mind. The buggy is this way."

Later, he would take time to remember what the lawyer had said, but for now, he had to take Faith Glick back to her grandfather's farm.

A grandfather she had never met.

Anger pushed its way through the grief, but as soon as Faith climbed into the buggy beside him, Gabriel knew he wouldn't be able to be angry for long. Faith looked like an angel. Her beauty was innocent and untouched. Her smile was sweet and kind—just like Levi's. He wouldn't allow her beauty to fool him.

Just like he wouldn't allow himself to accept that she was the most beautiful woman he'd ever met.

He took the reins and called to the horse. Perhaps when they reached the farm, he'd feel a little steadier.

Only the farm wasn't just his, it was now theirs.

# Chapter 3
# A Grievous Buggy Ride

If it hadn't been for her mother insisting, Faith would've never boarded the bus to Lancaster County. But ever since the Englisch lawyer saw them, her mother kept insisting that Faith couldn't ignore her heritage or her inheritance.

Her sweetheart, Isaac Yoder, had been devastated to hear that she must travel to Lancaster County. His response to her news had been the same as Faith's: what was she going to do with half a farm in Lancaster County?

If it was up to Faith, she would've forgotten about the lawyer's visit and happily continued with her life. She had a steady income as Daniel's babysitter. Isaac had been courting her for three months and although they hadn't even held hands, Faith was sure it was only a matter of time before her heart fluttered and swelled with affection for her childhood friend.

She respected her mother's wishes and was grateful that her grandfather had thought of her in his last will and testament, but that didn't mean it elated Faith about leaving her life behind to come to a state she'd never even considered visiting.

Last night before she boarded the bus, her mother had pulled her aside with a tearful look. "I know you don't want to go; I understand that. But understand this, Faith. They arranged my marriage to your daed. I have never and never will regret that, but I regret leaving my childhood community. This is a way for you to have something of my childhood, to see where I came from and to learn a little more about the life I lived before coming to Ohio."

Faith had hugged her mother and promised to do just that, although she wasn't sure how she was going to learn anything since her only relative in Lancaster County had been buried the week before.

She glanced at the man who had picked her up and wondered who he was. He had expected her mother and had seemed more than a little perturbed when Faith had explained to him who she was.

He couldn't be family since her grandfather had been her only living relative in this community. Which begged the question, who was he?

"How long is the drive to the farm?" Faith asked as the town buildings tapered away and fields appeared in the distance.

"About thirty minutes," Gabriel said plainly.

The lawyer had told her that Gabriel Lapp would come and collect her, but he said nothing more about the man sitting beside her. Faith considered waiting until she could ask the lawyer, but since she wasn't sure when that would be, she turned to Gabriel with a questioning look.

"I'm sorry, but who are you? The lawyer mentioned you'd be coming to collect me from the bus stop, but I'm not sure where... who... how..." The words faded from her mind when Gabriel turned to her.

His hair was the color of coffee when you added just a touch of cream. His eyes, a light brown, hazel even. Right now, those hazel eyes were looking straight at her.

Faith felt a rush of electricity race through her body unexpectedly.

"I inherited the other half," Gabriel stated bluntly.

Faith's brow furrowed. "You... We..." Her mind was spinning so fast she couldn't seem to finish a coherent sentence. It had to be that, because it simply couldn't be Gabriel's hazel eyes that had robbed her of speech.

"Levi left half of his property to me in his will, and the other half to you," Gabriel explained. He let out a quiet sigh and turned his gaze to the dirt road ahead. "He was like a father to me..."

"I don't know what to say. Are we familye?" Faith asked, wondering if her mother might have forgotten about an aunt or uncle that might still be around.

"Nee." Gabriel shook his head. "My parents died when I was seven. It was a buggy accident and before I knew it, I was an orphan. At the time there wasn't anyone in the community willing to adopt me, so I was taken by the Englisch to social services."

"I'm sorry, that sounds terrible. It must have been devastating for you." Faith couldn't help but sympathize. She couldn't imagine losing her parents and being taken away from everything she knew and loved.

"It was. But the following morning Levi showed up and told me to get my things. He took me to the farm and sat me down on the porch as if I was his equal and not a little boy. He offered to take me in as my guardian—if I wanted. I haven't left the farm since." Gabriel's voice softened with a smile. "The farm is the only home I've ever known."

Although he didn't say it, Faith could hear the accusation in his voice. The farm was his home, his inheritance, and she was nothing but an intruder that hadn't even met her grandfather. "He sounds like he was a kind man."

"The kindest. He raised me with a firm hand. Always made sure my homework was done on time and always made sure that I knew that I was loved." Gabriel's voice broke. "I'm sorry, I miss him. Not that you would understand."

"It's not my fault I hadn't met him," Faith quickly defended herself.

"Nee, it isn't. It's just been a long week and a hard one at that. I know you have just as much right to be there as I do." Gabriel apologized with a small smile.

"I can see you feel that I'm imposing in some way, but I want to assure you that isn't my intention at all. My mamm insisted I came, at least to see her childhood home and to put flowers on my grosspappi's grave," Faith explained.

"You must be tired after the long journey?" Gabriel changed the subject.

Faith nodded as a large farmhouse came into view. "Jah. I can't believe how long it took to get here by bus. I can only imagine how long it must take with a buggy."

"Well, we're almost there. The house is right up ahead." Gabriel pointed to the farmhouse.

Faith felt a smile curve her mouth. The house was beautiful, almost as if it belonged in a story book. There was a large red barn behind it, and around it fields as far as the eye could see. "It's beautiful."

"It's home," Gabriel stated simply as he turned into the yard.

Faith glanced at him from the corner of her eye and couldn't help but feel sympathy for the man she barely knew. Although he wasn't related to her grandfather, it was clear he was grieving from the loss. And to add to his grief, here she was claiming her half of the farm.

A half she still didn't know what she wanted to do with.

# Chapter 4
# Down Memory Lane

Gabriel stopped the buggy in front of the barn and knew he had to rethink the whole situation. He had expected Levi's daughter, an older woman, not his granddaughter. It had already been uncomfortable for him to share a house with Levi's married daughter, but to share a house with his unmarried granddaughter would be completely unacceptable.

He glanced up at the hayloft and knew it was the only solution at hand.

Faith climbed out of the buggy and lifted her face to sun. "It's gut to be back on a farm after spending so many hours traveling. The fresh air alone seems to have recuperated me."

When she turned to him with a smile, Gabriel felt his heart skip a beat. Her cheeks had a touch of color to them, a smile beaming on her pretty face.

"Let me show you to the house," Gabriel said gruffly before collecting her luggage.

As if in a dream, Faith looked at the house as if it were an apparition. "This is where my mamm grew up... it's hard to imagine her anywhere but at our home, in Ohio."

Gabriel waited a moment for her to reminisce.

He watched her walk to the kitchen garden and couldn't help but smile when she bent down to touch the ground. She looked up at him with dirt in her hands a grin on her face. "This is probably where she planted her first herbs and vegetables."

"Probably," Gabriel shrugged. He needed to remember why she was here and to stop thinking about how she made him feel. His heart wasn't thinking straight at the moment, he reminded himself. He felt nothing for this stranger. It was merely the grief, surprise, and loss all mingling together and confusing him. "Kùmm, let's get you settled in."

Faith dusted her hands and followed him onto the porch. Gabriel opened the door, grateful that he'd made a little effort with dusting and cleaning the day before.

Faith chuckled softly behind him. "I think she literally tried to create this home in Ohio. The furniture isn't exactly the same, but the layout... It's exactly like home." Without waiting for Gabriel to comment, Faith rushed towards the kitchen and opened the cupboard beside the woodstove. Laughter bubbled from her throat as he walked into the kitchen. "Even the cups and saucers are in the same place."

Gabriel nodded, not sure how to respond. He set down her luggage and took off his wide brim hat. "I put fresh linens on the spare bed for you."

"Denke, I would've taken care of that myself." Faith assured him as she filled the kettle with water. "Kaffe? I'm dying for some."

Gabriel nodded, admiring how at ease she was within minutes of entering his home. "Denke."

"Which room is yours?" Faith asked, turning to him before her eyes widened with surprise.

"Don't worry, I'll take the hayloft while you're here. I was expecting your mamm, not you. Otherwise, it would've been understandable," Gabriel explained.

"I don't want to put you out. This is your home. I'll take the hayloft," Faith offered eagerly.

"Nee," Gabriel said firmly. "If Levi knew I took the house and put you in the hayloft, he'd come back from the grave to teach me some manners." Just saying Levi's name hurt.

"I can see he meant a lot to you. I'm sure you meant a lot to him as well," Faith said kindly.

"He didn't have anyone, and neither did I," Gabriel said simply.

"But you had each other, that's all that matters. I can't remember the number of times my mamm wanted to bring me for a visit over the years. But every time she wrote to my grosspappi, he returned a letter stating that she needed to be home to care for her husband. That it would be an unnecessary expense." Faith sighed with a shake of her head. "I just never thought he'd be gone before..."

"It happened suddenly, none of us could've known," Gabriel said, remembering that morning.

"If I might ask, the lawyer didn't say how..." Faith trailed off with a questioning look.

"He had a heart attack in his sleep. Doctor said it would've been over before he knew what was happening. A blessing, really. Especially for someone of his age," Gabriel repeated the doctor's words.

Their gazes met and held and, for the first time in his life, Gabriel felt off balance. It was as if his steady world had just shifted beneath him. As if he couldn't for the life of him hang onto anything except Faith's blue eyes.

He was twenty-eight years old and had taken a few girls on buggy rides in the past, but he'd experienced nothing like this before. He cleared his throat and stepped towards the door. "I'll start gathering what I'll need for the hayloft."

"Please, let me help. I feel terrible for putting you out," Faith said, stepping forward.

"Nee, I've got it. If you want to help, try to help around the house. I've got enough work going on around the farm." His words were blunt, but he needed to cut himself off from her.

"Then I'll start on dinner," Faith offered with a smile. "But first, kaffe."

Gabriel nodded before he turned and walked towards his own bedroom. He muttered as he packed some clothes, toiletries, and a few other items into a bag. If it had disappointed him when he learned Levi hadn't left him the farm, he was now furious that Levi hadn't told him about his granddaughter.

Because having Faith Glick on the farm was going to be harder than to accept Levi's absence.

# Chapter 5
# No Room for Dessert

Faith hadn't thought she would feel so comfortable in a home she hadn't ever been in before, but something about her grandfather's house felt familiar. As if the memories of her mother's childhood still lingered in the hallway.

She had unpacked her things and opened the windows to air out the bedroom that Gabriel had made up for her. Considering two men had lived here for the last twenty years, she was surprised by how clean and dust-free the entire house was.

When she had finished unpacking, she found herself restless with fatigue. She was too excited about exploring her mother's heritage to rest after her journey, so instead started on dinner. Faith found a beef roast in the freezer and some vegetables in the pantry and indulged in the simple task of cooking. Every time she had finished a dish and realized that it would be some time before Gabriel would be around for dinner, she started on the next one.

By the time Gabriel stepped into the kitchen, shortly before six o'clock, she had cooked an entire feast. The kitchen table was laid with dish after dish of vegetables, and she had even made a dessert.

"When I meant you could help around the house, I didn't expect this?" Gabriel's surprise made her smile.

"Don't fret. I won't be cooking like this every night. I'm too tired to rest, so I cooked instead. Besides, when's the last time you had a meal like this?" Faith asked with a cocked brow and a hand on her hip.

Gabriel glanced at the peas, carrots, squash, rice, roast, potatoes, corn, and beans and let out a heavy sigh. "Honestly?"

"Honestly," Faith nodded.

"I don't think I've ever had a meal like this. Levi and I usually stuck to meat and potatoes with the odd vegetable on the side." Gabriel shrugged.

Faith smiled, feeling pleased. His gratitude for the meal eased her guilt about him staying in the hayloft. "Gut, then, let's eat before it gets cold."

They sat down and instinctually, Faith held out her hand. Although they were both Amish, the dinner time prayers differed from household to household. In Faith's home, they always held hands and said grace out loud.

Gabriel glanced at her hand and hesitated for a moment before taking it.

Faith closed her eyes, fearing he would see the surprise in her eyes. It felt different holding Gabriel's hand than it did when she held her father's.

She waited for him to say grace as the head of the household, but when he didn't speak, Faith took the liberty to say grace herself. "Denke Gott, for the nourishment we will receive and for the blessings you have bestowed upon us this day. Amen."

Gabriel let her hand go and instantly Faith missed it. She quickly snuck it under the table and rubbed her hand to rub away the memory of how her hand had felt in his. She thought of Isaac and wondered why she didn't feel that way with him.

They ate in silence, but Faith smiled now and then when Gabriel helped himself to more. When he had finished almost three plates, she couldn't help but laugh. "I can't decide if you were hungry or if you simply enjoyed the meal?"

Gabriel's smiled held a touch of guilt. "Both? It's the best meal I've ever had. You truly have a talent for cooking."

"If you think that, you clearly haven't tasted my mamm's cooking," Faith said as she cleared their plates.

"How is she? Your mamm?" Gabriel's eyes were curious as they met hers.

A smile curved the corners of Faith's mouth. "Gut; healthy, happy. She's a gut mamm."

"Levi often spoke fondly of his memories of her as a child. Am I right they sent her to Ohio to meet the agreement of an arranged marriage?"

"Jah," Faith confirmed. "And to this day, she doesn't regret it. It was a match made by Gott himself, Mamm insists."

"She must be very sad that you left?" Gabriel continued his gentle interrogation.

"Jah, she was. But I understand why she wanted me to come. I never expected to be included in Levi's will. Neither did she."

"And now that you are… do you intend to stay here?" Gabriel's voice lowered and the smile on his face disappeared.

Faith tilted her head, only now realizing how much he was bothered by her part in her grandfather's will. "I don't know. I don't know what I'm going to do. My whole life is in Ohio. My… I can't imagine staying here."

"Then let's make this simple. Let me buy you out. I'll buy your half of the farm. I won't be able to pay you immediately, but I can pay you back. We can work out an arrangement and I promise I'll make it worth your while," Gabriel said urgently.

Faith frowned, surprised by his offer. "You're very generous, Gabriel, but why would you want to do that?"

Gabriel sighed heavily and glanced around the kitchen. "Because I can't imagine myself leaving. If you're not planning on staying, that means you're selling. And if you sell to someone else, I lose my half as well."

"You'll get your half of the money," Faith insisted.

"It's my home, Faith, please… don't sell my home," Gabriel all but pleaded.

"I… I don't know what I'm going to do. I just know that my mamm wanted me to come here. Let me think about it for a few days. Perhaps then… I'll know what I want to do," Faith explained.

Gabriel nodded before he stood up from the table. "I don't think I have room for dessert."

Before Faith could tempt him to have a slice of her pecan pie, the screen door slammed shut. A heaviness settled over her shoulders, realizing that she hadn't just inherited half a farm, indirectly she had also inherited the fate of Gabriel's future.

Faith wasn't sure that was a weight she wanted to carry.

# Chapter 6
# Humor & Eggs

Gabriel had barely slept a wink the night before. He had honestly thought that whoever his co-inheritor was from Ohio, they would eagerly accept his offer to buy them out. But Faith didn't seem all that eager to fall for his suggestion. Which meant it left him exactly where he had been the morning before.

Unsure of what the future would bring.

The only difference this morning was that he was sleeping in a hayloft, while a beautiful woman was sleeping in his home. He pushed himself up and yawned. Sleep was an integral part of every farmer's day; without it, productivity would simply dwindle. But unless Faith accepted his offer, he knew he wouldn't get a good night's rest.

He needed a plan; he realized, once he was dressed and ready for the day.

A smile curved his mouth by the time he headed to the kitchen for breakfast and coffee. The quickest way to get Faith to accept his offer was to make her see why he wanted to buy her out. Perhaps if he showed her the farm and showed her why it was important to him, she wouldn't insist on selling to a stranger. Perhaps then she would agree to his terms, sign a contract, and go back home to Ohio.

"Guten mayrie," Faith greeted brightly when he stepped into the kitchen. Gabriel had expected her to still be fast asleep.

"Guten mayrie," Gabriel greeted her as he helped himself to coffee. "How did you sleep?"

"Very well." Faith smiled at him as she took a seat at the table. "Would you like me to cook you breakfast?"

Gabriel couldn't help but find her offer endearing. He'd never had someone offer him breakfast before. "Nee, but denke. I usually just grab an apple."

Faith gasped with horror. "Not anymore." She was out of her chair and by the stove in a matter of minutes. "If you don't want a big breakfast, then at least some scrambled eggs and toast."

Before Gabriel could argue, she had already cracked two eggs in the pan.

"A sturdy breakfast is the best beginning to everyday. What are your plans for today?" Faith asked as she moved the eggs with a spatula.

"I uhm…" Gabriel was lost in his own thoughts for a moment. It felt strange to sit in the kitchen early morning while a woman cooked him breakfast.

It didn't feel strange, it was nice.

"I actually thought of giving you a tour of the farm. Showing you the different fields, the different crops we grow on each. Maybe if the weather isn't too cool, I could show you the creek."

"There's a creek?" Faith asked excitedly as she loaded the eggs onto toast.

"Jah, we swim in it when the days are hot in summer. Do you have a creek back home?"

Faith shook her head. "Nee, but we have a large dam. Sometimes when it's very hot, a few of my girlfriends and I will sneak off and swim. The mud is squishy between your toes, but the water is so nice and cool you hardly notice."

Gabriel laughed at her description. "The creek has rocks, so no squishy mud."

"That's a relief." Faith cracked another two eggs and began making herself the same breakfast. "I didn't expect to like it here, but it's nice. Last night I got up in the middle of the night and realized I was all alone. I waited for the fear coming, but it didn't."

"Are you usually afraid?" Gabriel asked with a questioning look. The eggs were fluffy and perfectly seasoned. For a moment he considered begging her to stay just for her cooking. He wouldn't even mind moving into the hayloft if she did.

"Nee, not at all. But strange town, strange community, strange house..." Faith trailed off. She took a seat at the table and met his gaze with a questioning look. "Tell me about Levi. What was he like? What were his days like?"

Gabriel smiled fondly at the affectionate memory of Eli. "He was the best man I've ever known. He used to have more energy than I did, but he slowed down a little over these last few years."

"His age was probably slowing him down." Faith nodded with understanding. She could see her own parents slow down.

"Jah. He would join me in the fields in the morning, but after lunch he'd take to the porch. You see that rocker out there, he'd snooze in it all afternoon, pretending to be watching me." Gabriel chuckled even as grief touched his heart.

"Was he funny? I mean, did he make jokes or tease at all?" Faith rested her chin on her hand.

Gabriel laughed. "Jah, how did you know?"

"My mamm. She has a great sense of humor. She has a way of making you laugh when you least expect it. Even when she was saying goodbye to me at the bus station. She teased me about forgetting about Ohio altogether. That would *never* happen." Faith smiled.

Gabriel nodded, but he wished her mother had just been teasing. The last thing he needed was for Faith to fall in love with the farm and Lancaster County.

Then he might as well say goodbye to his plans of buying her out altogether.

# Chapter 7
## Eden

Faith had only known the farmlands of Ohio her entire life. The wide-open spaces and big skies had captured her imagination from a young age. On her bus journey from Ohio to Pennsylvania, she had seen numerous landscapes and had held fast to her love for Ohio.

But it had only taken a tour of her grandfather's farm to make her realize that Lancaster County held its own appeal. The lush green rolling hills and tall trees were different and yet beautiful at the same time. White houses dotted the Amish community, buggies travelling on the dirt roads while children played in the yard.

Faith hadn't known what to expect when she arrived in Lancaster County and now she couldn't help but feel as if she were home. A different home. One where the landscape and the people were new to her, but welcome hung in the air.

Gabriel had taken her on a tour of the entire farm. He had shown her every field, explained to her every crop he would sow, and what harvests he expected to reap. As they walked along the fence line to a copse of trees in the distance, Faith listened to him talk.

It was the excitement in his eyes and his tone of voice that held her attention more than the words. Even if she hadn't heard a single word, she would've understood that Gabriel loved this farm. He didn't lie when he had said it was home. He spoke with so much determination and hope for the future that Faith found herself even more confused about what she was going to do.

If she wanted to sell her half, then it would be wrong of her to sell it to anyone but Gabriel. She would take away his dreams.

Faith still didn't know what she was going to do, and although it was only her second day on the farm, she knew she had to decide soon. She couldn't dwindle time in Lancaster County, keeping both her family and Gabriel on the edge of their seats, waiting for her decision.

A decision that would affect every single one of them.

Especially Isaac.

A frown creased her brow as Isaac came to mind. A few days ago, she had been certain that she wanted to spend her future with Isaac, but she only realized now she hadn't thought of him once. Guilt washed over her before she convinced herself something had merely distracted her with the journey and arriving on her grandfather's farm.

"Something wrong?" Gabriel stopped and turned to her with a questioning look.

Faith shook her head and smiled. "Nee. I was just wondering if Isaac would've thought it's as beautiful here as I do. Just like me, Ohio is all he's ever known."

"Is it much different there?" Gabriel asked, picking a twig of grass and twiddling it between his fingers.

"I accept the community is much the same, seeing as we're all Amish," Faith answered with a smile. "But the landscape… it is different. It's not as green and there aren't as many hills. And trees, the trees here are different–more and bigger."

"Do you like it?" Gabriel asked curiously.

Faith paused for a moment before her smile broadened. "How can I not?"

"Kumm, you haven't seen the creek yet." Gabriel began walking again.

Faith laughed as she fell into step beside him. "Have you ever been anywhere else?"

"Harrisburg for my Rumspringa, but I came home after just a few days. Too many people in the city," Gabriel explained.

"I can't imagine going to the city for rumspringa. A few of my friends did, but I stayed at home. I didn't need to see what I was missing to know that I was Amish in my heart." Faith stumbled over a rock and Gabriel quickly grabbed her arm.

"Are you alright?" Gabriel asked, holding on until he was sure she was steady.

Faith blushed. "I'm fine. That's what happens when you talk too much and don't look where you're going."

She stepped out of his embrace, wondering why his hand on her arm had made a current of energy jolt straight into her tummy.

"Just through those trees and we'll be there." Gabriel smiled over his shoulder, leading the way.

They walked in silence for a while until Faith gasped with awe. *"This* is your creek?"

Gabriel nodded triumphantly. "Quite the Eden, isn't it?"

Faith glanced around with admiration. A creek curved its way over rocks and around bends until it reached a slight fall. The waterfall was only about two feet high, but the water happily plunged onto the rocks in the small pool below. If she had to guess, the pool was about four feet deep and about as large as two buggies standing side by side.

The water was crystal clear with just a few rays of sun making it through the trees that covered the pool. "It's... magnificent. You must have lived here as a kinner. I can't imagine wanting to be anywhere else on a hot summer's day."

"I did and, to be honest, even now, I sneak off on hot days to cool off," Gabriel laughed, kicking off his shoes and sitting on the edge of the pool with his feet in the water.

For a moment Faith considered keeping her decorum intact before laughter bubbled from her throat and she kicked off her shoes as well. She sat down on a large rock with her feet dangling over the edge in the cool water. "I wonder if Isaac would believe me if I told him about this. I wish I could snap a memory and share it with him when I get home."

"Isaac, is he... your friend?" Gabriel asked, keeping his gaze on the rays of sun dancing on the water as morning turned to noon.

Faith only now realized that she had been talking about Isaac on and off and hadn't even explained who he is. "Nee, he's my... beau."

Faith had never had to explain Isaac's presence in her life to anyone, as everyone back home knew they were courting, but to use the word beau felt like such an enormous commitment.

"So you're courting, then?" Gabriel splashed up some water with his feet into the middle of the pool.

"Jah. For a few months." Faith laughed when some of the water splashed onto her.

"Then I can imagine you don't want to spend too much time in Lancaster County. You're probably eager to get home?" Gabriel asked with a look that Faith couldn't quite place.

She thought of his question and knew that her answer should be undoubtedly yes, but for some reason she wanted to stay here just a little longer in this beautiful county with its rolling hills and tall trees.

"Nee, I don't want to be away for too long," she finally answered, wondering if Gabriel could hear the doubt in her words.

Something about this place, about the man beside her, made her feel as if Ohio was a world away. She wasn't sure what or why, but she just knew she wasn't ready to go back home just yet.

At least not until she figured out why this place called to her and why Gabriel made her heart skip a beat and her mind spin.

# Chapter 8
# A Blood Curdling Scream

After their tour of the farm, Gabriel had felt something grow inside him he'd never experienced before. Telling Faith about his dreams for the future and his hopes for the farm. He had felt a connection with her he hadn't ever expected.

For the first time since learning about Levi's will, he didn't feel as if Faith were an intruder, instead, she had felt like his ally.

Until she had mentioned Isaac.

Jealousy had snapped at his heart and the feeling had been so unfamiliar that at first, Gabriel hadn't been sure what it was. Until she continued to talk about Isaac by the pool. He wasn't supposed to like Faith, but hearing her talk about her sweetheart had made him wish he could be her sweetheart instead.

Confused and more than a little surprised by the powerful attraction he felt for Faith, he knew it would be wise to keep his distance. There was the farm at stake, and he didn't need to offend her by acting on his attraction, only to lose the farm altogether.

He knew that if they sold the farm, he would get a handsome amount to buy a smaller place of his own. But

Gabriel didn't want another farm. He wanted the one he called home.

Ever since then, for the last three days, he had kept his distance from her. He joined her for mealtimes, but the rest of the day he spent working on the farm. He was tilling the fields before he could plow them for sowing, and the hard work made him tired in the evenings.

By the time he fell into bed in the hayloft, he barely had time to think before he fell asleep.

Gabriel had felt grounded for most of his life. He remembered after losing his parents he felt a little uncertain of what the future would bring, but Levi had soon eased his fears when he had taken him in. Now, for the first time in years, he found himself a little off balance again.

Losing Levi had been very hard. Levi had fulfilled so many roles in his life that it was hard to imagine going on without him. Levi had been both his mother and father, his grandfather, his role model, his friend, and his mentor on the farm.

For Gabriel, it still felt as if he had lost six loved ones instead of one.

He was still trying to deal with the grief and to move on without Levi there to give him guidance and now he was overcome with more uncertain emotions.

Faith wasn't anything like he expected her to be. From the moment he had set eyes on her, he had known that she was special.

The special that could sneak into your heart and stay there.

Just when he had thought something good might come of her visit to Ohio, he learned about her Isaac. Gabriel didn't want to envy another man, his girl. Just like he didn't want to lose his heart for the first time on a girl he could never have.

It felt as if it didn't matter in which direction he tried to move. There were rocks around him that kept tripping him, no matter how hard he tried.

So he focused on the work. Gabriel was doing his afternoon chores in the barn, wondering how much longer it would take for Faith to decide and return to Ohio, when he suddenly heard a blood-curdling scream coming from the house.

Before he knew it, his instinct had him running to the house as if it were on fire. He rushed up the porch, taking the steps two at a time, fearing something dreadful had happened to Faith. The front door was all but swinging off his hinges as he burst through. A single glance at the living room revealed Faith wasn't there, making Gabriel rush towards the kitchen.

As soon as he set a foot through the door, a frown creased his brow even as his heart slowed down a little to see her safe. There wasn't a single drop of blood on her. She was standing on her feet and seemingly in perfect health.

But she was on the table.

Her eyes were wide as she looked at him with gratitude. "Thanks heavens you came!"

"Came for what? You were screaming as if someone were about to slice your head off." Gabriel looked up at her with an irritable expression.

# Chapter 9
# Listen to your heart

Faith's heart was still racing a mile a minute as she looked down into Gabriel's dark eyes. "I was scared. That's what women do when they're terrified!"

"Of what?" Gabriel teased with a cocked brow. "Of the chairs?"

He glanced at the overturned chair on the floor and chuckled. "Let me guess, it was following you?"

Faith hated that he was teasing her, but she wouldn't let him humiliate her. "The chair had nothing to do with it." She cocked her hands on her hips and drew in a deep breath as she pointed towards the pantry. "I was in there cleaning the pantry since I saw the top shelves had about an inch of dust on them. I was standing on that chair." She pointed at the chair. "Then suddenly, out of nowhere, something slithered over my hand. I jumped off the chair and ran to the table. It was a snake!" she ended defiantly.

Gabriel frowned, shaking his head. "All this fuss over a snake. How big?"

"About this long." Faith held her hands a few inches apart.

"What type of snake was it?" Gabriel asked, already sounding bored with the subject, making Faith only angrier.

"Since I was running for my life and jumping onto the table, I didn't consider stopping to ask its name! It went that way!" she pointed to the backdoor.

"Gut, then it's gone." Gabriel shrugged as if it was nothing.

"It was here! What if there's another one?" Faith asked, doubting if she'd ever climb off the table.

"If it was this big and brownish, it was a house snake. It eats rats, not humans," Gabriel explained with a teasing grin. "Maybe your hand looked like a rat.... Nee, I'm sure you just frightened it by moving things around."

"Does that mean you have rats in the pantry?" Faith cried out, mortified.

"Not anymore, if the snake was there." Gabriel poured himself a glass of water. "We live on a farm. Snakes have a way of finding their way inside, just like they have a way of finding their way outside again. I've never seen a poisonous snake on this farm, and I can promise you neither will you."

He drank down his water before setting down the glass. "Now, would you like me to help you down or would you like to stay up there for the rest of the day?"

Faith hesitated for a moment. "I'm not sure. Don't you just want to check the shelves in the pantry first?" she asked with a small voice, making Gabriel laugh.

He humored her by stepping into the pantry and running his hands over all the shelves, one by one. When he was done, he turned to her with a questioning look. "There, happy?"

"Happy nee, but I feel better knowing that you checked."

Gabriel stepped forward and held out his hands. Faith rested her hands on his shoulders, and he swiftly picked her off the table and set her down.

As soon as her feet hit the floor, Faith looked up and into Gabriel's warm brown eyes. His hands were still on her hips and her heart was racing again. But this time not with fear for a snake, but with... anticipation.

Standing this close to him, she could see the hazel and gold specks in his eyes. He no longer seemed irate that she had cried out like a banshee, instead, he looked as intrigued by her as she was by him.

Gabriel's breathing grew a little shallower, even as Faith's body warmed beneath his gaze. She had once heard a friend explain how it felt when you were in love and hated that she felt this way with Gabriel, yet she couldn't seem to get herself to move away. Something about Gabriel wanted her to step closer.

Somewhere in the back of her mind, she remembered Isaac, but she couldn't ever remember feeling this way when Isaac was near.

Gabriel suddenly stepped back and cleared his throat. "There, you're safe now. Next time, just take a broom and sweep it out."

Faith's laughter was filled with disbelief. "You want me to sweep out a snake?"

"That's what Levi and I did." Gabriel shrugged. "Oh, I forgot to tell you there came a letter for you this morning." His eyes darkened and Faith felt the distance between them grow, although neither of them had moved again.

"There did? Is it from Ohio?" Faith asked hopefully, trying to ease her heart that was struggling to find a normal beat again.

"Jah. I put it on the server in the dining room," Gabriel said briskly before he started towards the door.

Faith couldn't help but be confused by his teasing affection one moment and his cold disinterest the next. "Denke."

She let out a giant sigh of relief when Gabriel's footsteps faded. "Gott, please help me understand what's going on. I don't want to betray Isaac...."

The words had barely left her mouth when she noticed Gabriel standing in the door. Her face flushed bright pink, not knowing how much he had heard or hadn't heard. "I uhm..."

"I just wanted to tell you I'm going to see the lawyer tomorrow. I think it's in our best interest if he can get us out of this co-inheritor business. Maybe there's a clause, or something similar he can use..." Gabriel trailed off.

"Gut, I'm coming with," Faith said quickly. "I've been meaning to see him since I arrived. What time will we be leaving?"

Faith could see that her answer had caught Gabriel off guard. "I'll phone from the shanty later today to make an appointment. I'll tell you tonight."

Just like that, Gabriel turned and left. Faith waited until she heard his footsteps disappear and glanced out the window to make sure he was gone this time before she let out her sigh.

With Isaac, her interactions had always been so easy. He'd make a joke, and she'd laugh. Or when he was having a bad day, she would cheer him. She never had to wonder what Isaac was thinking, but with Gabriel it was as if he had a lock on his mind and no one could get through it.

One moment she thought she saw kindness and understanding, only to feel brushed aside the next.

Faith wished her mother had been here to give her advice, or at least to keep her company, but her mother was in Ohio.

And when Faith would return, she wasn't sure.

She turned to the only other source of comfort and guidance that she had: Gott.

She stood by the window and looked out over the fields as she prayed. *"Gott, please help me understand why you brought me here. Why would my grosspappi leave me half a farm? I know it's my heritage, but Ohio is my home. Why did you want me to come here? I can feel there is a greater plan with all this, but I can't see what it is. Should I stay and wait for you to guide me, or should I simply return home to Isaac and my familye? Help me understand why Gabriel makes me feel so different from Isaac does. Please Gott, I feel as if I'm being swallowed by Kudzu vines and I don't have a knife to cut me free. Guide me, lead me, and let me make the right decisions for everyone involved. Help me know what I need to do. Help me do it to earn your blessings. Amen."*

In the distance, she saw Gabriel walking from the barn to the fields and a bible verse came to mind. Until that moment, Faith hadn't ever heard it before. It was as if Gott had whispered it into her ear. The verse was so powerful that she rushed to her room to check if it actually existed in the bible. She flicked through the pages until she found it and her heart simply stopped. Was this Gott's way of answering her prayers? She read the verse again, following it word by word as it had come to her in her mind.

*Ephesians 4:2 Be completely humble and gentle; be patient and bearing with one another in love.*

The only question she had now was, did the verse refer to her and Isaac?

Or her and Gabriel?

# Chapter 10
# Legal Jargon

The following morning, Gabriel was on his way to town without even stopping by the house for breakfast first. His tummy growled, not impressed with his decision at all. But Gabriel wanted to see the lawyer and get some answers before he saw Faith again.

Yesterday, when he'd walked into the kitchen and seen her up on the table, she had looked so adorable. His heart had swelled with affection, imagining how fun a life with Faith would be. It had only taken him a moment to remember that dreams like that weren't suitable.

Faith was already taken.

Her heart belonged to a man named Isaac that lived in Ohio.

Gabriel had lost sleep last night over a man he'd never met before. He wondered what Isaac was like. Was he kind, was he caring, could he provide for Faith? Did Faith truly love him, or was it a match that her parents had orchestrated?

The more he thought about Isaac, the more the guilt had overwhelmed him.

Faith was nothing more to him than a co-inheritor of Levi's property. She wasn't his future and the sooner he accepted that, the better.

He stopped by the diner and ordered a cup of coffee and breakfast to kill time until his appointment with the lawyer. While he sat in the diner, he saw a few girls from his community laughing in a booth across from him. All of them were single and eligible to be courted. Why couldn't he like one of them instead?

His heart felt heavy knowing that when he bought Faith out, she might be out of his way and out of sight, but it would take much longer for him to get her out of his heart.

A heavy sigh escaped him as he paid the bill. He made his way out of the diner towards the lawyer's offices. Hopefully, the lawyer would've found a clause by now that would make it possible for Gabriel to buy Faith out.

Levi had taught him that loans were an added weight to life. And if you didn't keep an eye on your course, it would weigh down a sinking ship even faster. But if a loan meant he could keep the farm and focus on his future, then he would do everything in his power to keep his eyes on the course ahead and not on Levi's granddaughter that threatened to steal his heart and compromise his moral compass.

He was shown in to the lawyer's office and took a seat across from Mr. Anderson with an expectant look. "Guten Mayrie, Mr. Anderson."

"Gabriel, it's good to see you. I've been looking into the matter you asked of me when we last spoke," Mr. Anderson said, opening a file.

"And? Have you found a clause or a way for me to buy Faith out sooner than the required month?" Gabriel asked hopefully.

Mr. Anderson let out a heavy sigh. "I'm afraid that won't be possible. But something else has come to my attention. While I was going through the files trying to find a previous will, or an additional clause, I found these." He handed Gabriel an envelope. "There was one for me, one for you, and this one is for Faith."

"What are they?" Gabriel asked, recognizing Levi's writing on the envelope.

"Letters. Since they were included with the will, I need to adhere to them as part of the last will and testament of Levi Stoltzfus," Mr. Anderson explained.

"What do you mean?" Gabriel asked, opening his letter.

"The letter Levi left me clarified that before either your or Faith may buy each other out, you need to live on the farm for one month together. That means that I can't even begin drawing up the contracts until the requested period has passed." Mr. Anderson said with a shrug. "I'm sorry I didn't find these sooner. We installed new office furniture a few months ago. They must have been misplaced then."

"What if I don't want to wait? What if Faith wants to go back to Is…? Ohio?" Gabriel asked with a heavy heart. He had hoped that he would get clarity this morning, not learn about more complications.

"Then you both lose. If you don't adhere to Levi's request, the assets and property will be bequeathed to the bishop for community use."

"Community use?" Gabriel cried out, baffled. "It makes little sense. None of this makes sense."

"Perhaps when you read the letter, it will. I have a client waiting, but if you don't want to lose your inheritance, Gabriel, I'll see you in thirty days."

"But four days have already passed?" Gabriel asked, confused.

"Today marks the first day as I've only now informed you of this request." Mr. Anderson stood up, making it clear their meeting was over.

Gabriel shook his hand before he left the lawyer's office and headed back to his buggy. As soon as he climbed in, he pulled out Levi's letter and read.

*My dearest Gabriel*

*If you are reading this, then it means that I am no longer with you. I want you to know that you were the son I never had. You were there when I had no one else. I can still remember the day I went to fetch you, how frightened you looked at this scraggly old man. Just like I can remember every moment you made my heart swell with love.*

*I love you, Gabriel, as if you were my own.*

*I can only hope that you cherished our relationship as much as I do.*

*The reason for this letter is simple. I'm sure by now you've learned that I have bequeathed the farm to and my granddaughter. I know this decision must confuse you, but I assure you it wasn't to anger or offend you.*

*Although I've never met Faith, I've learned from her mother that she is kind, patient, and gentle. I want her to know about her mother's heritage, to experience it for herself. There is no doubt in my mind that she'll return to Ohio after the thirty days are over. But just perhaps she finds something of herself in Lancaster County. I hope you can find it in your heart to share your heritage with her.*

*You've always made me proud, Gabriel, and I know you always will.*

*Warmest regards,*
*Levi*

# Chapter 11
# An Old Man's Request

Faith had considered going with Gabriel to see the attorney, but she wasn't sure riding in a buggy alone with Gabriel was such a good idea.

The way Gabriel made her feel confused, and she didn't need to be more confused now than she already was. Instead, she had stayed home and tended to the house chores. She wouldn't admit it, but it felt strange not to have Gabriel on the farm. It was her first time alone on the property where her mother had grown up on and although she wasn't afraid; she checked out the window every few minutes to see if Gabriel had returned yet.

It was shortly before lunch when Faith heard the horse's hooves gallop into the yard. She glanced out the window and felt her heart skip a beat at the sight of Gabriel. Surprised by how happy she was to see him, Faith quickly turned away from the window and busied herself by the stove.

"Hullo," Gabriel said as he walked into the kitchen a short while later.

"Hullo," Faith greeted him. "Kaffe?"

"Denke." Gabriel took a seat at the table with a heavy sigh.

Faith was bursting with curiosity over what the lawyer had said, but she knew it wasn't fitting for a woman to question a man. She poured him a cup of coffee and joined him at the kitchen table.

"I made a chicken pie for lunch," Faith filled the silence.

"It smells gut." Gabriel didn't seem too pleased by either her chicken pie or her presence. He drew in a deep breath and let it out on a sigh before he met Faith's gaze. "I'm afraid I don't have the best news."

"You don't?" Faith asked anxiously.

"Jah." Gabriel handed her an envelope. "I should've never asked the lawyer to dig a little deeper. Instead of finding a way for us to get out of this situation, he found more complications."

"Complications?" Faith asked, accepting the envelope.

"He found these letters that must have slipped out of Levi's will. One for me and one for you," Gabriel said heavily.

"What do they say?" Faith asked, glancing at the envelope.

"I don't know what yours says." Gabriel shrugged. "I can't buy you out and you can't sell the farm. We have to live here together for thirty days before we can even consider one of those options."

Faith gasped. "But I've already been here four days. I didn't plan on staying that long."

"Day one starts today," Gabriel said heavily.

"But... my parents... Isaac... This can't be true, can it? Could Levi even do that?" Faith asked, horrified.

"He did." Gabriel shrugged.

"So, what do we do now?" This was not the news Faith had hoped for.

"We make it through the thirty days."

"And if we don't?"

"Then we lose everything. They turn everything over to the bishop for the community's use. The fields as well," Gabriel said through clenched teeth.

Faith sighed and shook her head. "I... I have to write my familye."

"And Isaac," Gabriel's voice was sharp.

Faith met his gaze and knew that it had caught him just as off guard as she was by this fresh development. Strangely enough, the idea of spending another month with Gabriel didn't upset her. It was the thought of spending another month away from home.

And Isaac...

Faith wouldn't admit it, but with every day that she spent in Lancaster County, she found Isaac further and further from her mind.

"And Isaac," she confirmed before turning and walking out of the kitchen.

As soon as she was alone in her room, she opened the letter from her grandfather. A man she had never known that was now making demands on her time. She felt angry and more than a little upset, but she couldn't help but be curious about what he had to say to her.

*My dearest Faith*

*How I wish I could've met you. How I wish I could've heard your laughter and see your sweet face. But all things happen in accordance with Gott's will.*

*It was his will that took your mamm to Ohio and it was his will that you were raised there. But in my own way, an old man hoping to be remembered, I wanted a little of my family to return to Lancaster County in time.*

*Over the years, your mamm offered to come and visit many times, but I know, as a farmer, there are always unexpected costs.*

*I decided instead to let you come and remember me in another way. I wanted you to come and experience the farm, the town, and the community, and to remember me in the fields, the home, and the legacy I left behind.*

*I know you must be upset about the terms of my will, but I believe in my heart that a brief visit would never give you the opportunity to understand this old man's heart. Instead, the more time you spend here, the more you will learn about me, your mamm's childhood and how much this farm means to me.*

*You must be eager to return home, to your familye and your friends, but first I ask you to stay. Stay for thirty days.*

*Right now, you must be eager to sell your half of the property to Gabriel, and I can't say I blame you. But if you leave, Gabriel will lose his inheritance as well.*

*So for the sake of an old man's memory and a young man's dreams, use these thirty days to learn more about the grandfather you never knew and to appreciate the farm he loved all these years.*

*Perhaps, I might even be as bold as to say, you might fall in love with the farm and this community as well.*

*Although I've never held your hand or gazed into your eyes, which I've heard resembles your mamm's, I've always loved you and prayed for your wellbeing. Keep safe, my dearest Faith. Remain strong in faith and true to your heart and, most of all, remember to open your heart to opportunities you might find in the most unexpected places.*

*Perhaps even in Lancaster County.*

*Your doting grosspappi,*
*Levi*

The letter made little sense at all, Faith thought as she folded it and returned it to the envelope. She felt a little emotional knowing how much Levi had cared for her, but she wasn't sure what she would learn in thirty days that she hadn't learnt in three.

A few moments ago she had considered packing her bags and letting go not only of her inheritance, but any connection she might have to Levi Stoltzfus. Now she wasn't so sure. Could she really leave in haste and allow Gabriel to lose his future?

She remembered the bible verse from the day before and realized they had meant it for this moment. She needed to be patient.

With a sigh, she reached for a writing pad and a pen and wrote to her parents. She knew they would understand, seeing as it was family, but she wasn't so sure that Isaac would understand.

She wrote him a separate letter explaining the situation and asking him for both his patience and his trust until she returned.

When she was done, she walked to the mailbox. Once the letters were inside, she glanced out over the fields, wondering what she might find here that she had to open her heart to.

She saw Gabriel walking in the fields and spun away, because surely her grandfather hadn't meant Gabriel.

Or had he?

# Chapter 12
# An Angel's Voice

Over the last week, the bad weather had begun to build. Gabriel didn't need a forecast to know that a storm was brewing. One with thunder and lightning might even bring occasional flooding. It was a bit early in the year for thunderstorms, but that didn't stop Gabriel from making the precautions needed.

The drains around the house were dug open that would direct water away from the house to the fields. He checked the roof where it always leaked and even packed a few sandbags just inside the barn if he needed to stop water from coming in from under the door.

Since his visit to the attorney, Faith has been watching him from a distance. It was as if they had both retreated to themselves, knowing they had to spend the next month together.

Gabriel didn't mind having Faith around, but he minded the way his feelings for her were growing whenever they spent time together—which, at the moment, was only during meals.

The wind shifted and Faith's laundry on the line danced a wild rumba as it was whipped this way and that. She reached for a sheet just as her prayer kapp was carried off with the wind.

Her golden her hair tumbled from its braid as she tugged the sheets off the line. Gabriel dragged his gaze from her beauty to watch the thunder clouds darken overhead. The storm he had been waiting for was about to arrive.

The next hour was chaotic as he stabled horses in the barn, finished the day's chores, and took care of feeding and watering the animals. When the first fat drops of rain fell to the ground, kicking up dust, Gabriel ran towards the house for dinner.

Faith was standing by the window, almost mesmerized by the storm, when he walked in. "Isn't it magnificent?"

Gabriel shrugged as he shook the drops from his hat. "Jah, it is. But it's dangerous as well."

"I know. Are the animals safe?" Faith asked, turning to the two plates she had already filled with stew.

"Jah, all fed, watered and stabled for the night," Gabriel said, accepting his plate.

Faith set down her plate before she jumped almost as high as the table when the first crack of thunder made the windows shake. "It sounds like a big one."

"It is big," Gabriel agreed as he saw lightning dance in the sky.

They ate in silence, struggling to talk over the rain hammering against the tin roof while thunder roared overhead with the occasional crack that startled Faith every time. She barely touched her dinner, glancing out the window every few seconds with fear.

Gabriel had to resist the urge to reach for her hand to calm her down. He had never been afraid of storms before, but it was easy to see that they terrified Faith. "You're safe inside," he said when he stood up from the table.

"Ach, I know. I don't know why I'm afraid of storms. I always have been," Faith said, trying to make light of her fear.

"There are a lot of things we can't explain," Gabriel said, thinking of the feelings he had for Faith. "try to get some sleep."

He left the house before he did something foolish, like offering to stay with her for the night.

Gabriel had trouble falling asleep, as the storm hadn't only frightened Faith, but the horses as well. From his bed in the hayloft he could hear them puffing and groaning with fear even as one stomped its feet.

A few times he considered turning them out, to follow their instincts and run towards a shelter of their own choosing. But Gabriel knew they would only injure themselves. Fueled with adrenalin, they might step in a hole or run through a fence. Although they weren't happy, the barn was the safest place for them at the moment.

It felt as if he had just found rest in sleep when a loud roar of thunder woke him. As the sleep subsided, he heard the horses kick up a fuss downstairs. He pushed back the covers before he made his way down from the hayloft. He arrived at one stall just as their youngest mare was trying to kick down the door.

"Hush, hush, Peony," Gabriel said in soothing tones as he opened the door slowly and stepped inside. The horse's eyes were enormous with fear as she let out a loud nicker. It took him a while, but he finally reached her halter. He rubbed her neck in long slow strokes, trying to sooth her, but even his best efforts didn't seem to have an effect.

When the next bolt of lightning lit up the night, she kicked Gabriel away and reared up onto her back legs.

"It's okay, I'm here. I'm here now," Gabriel heard Faith's sweet voice from the stable door.

"Faith, don't. Gabriel crawled from the corner to avoid being trampled.

"She's not dangerous," Faith said softly as she stepped into the stall. "She's terrified. Aren't you girl?" Faith asked, moving towards the horse. She reached for the halter and didn't look at Gabriel a single time before she spoke. "I've got her. You get out of here Gabriel. See how badly you've been hurt."

Gabriel wanted to argue, but it seemed Faith's voice had a more soothing affect than Gabriel's had in the last ten minutes. He crawled out, feeling his side burning where the horse had kicked him. When he turned around, he watched Faith whispering to the horse.

"I know, Peony. I'm afraid of them as well. What do you say you and I keep each other company until it's over?" Faith asked with a sweet smile.

The horse nickered, but this time not in fear, almost in agreement.

"Faith, get out of there before the next lightning strikes," Gabriel urged her. He felt his own eyes widen with fear at seeing her with the horse.

Faith shook her head as she leaned back and convinced the horse to lie down. "There you go. The closer to the ground we are, the safer we are."

Gabriel couldn't believe his eyes. Faith was the closest thing to a horse whisperer he'd ever seen in his life. She sat with the horse, positioning its head on her lap as she sang a hymn from the ausband.

"Faith..." Gabriel pleaded again, but his plea fell on deaf ears.

When the next bolt of lightning lit up the barn, Faith sang a little louder, forcing herself not to show how afraid she was. Being strong for the horse made the horse calmer, although Gabriel could see Faith was just as afraid.

Finally, he sat down outside the stall and soon fell asleep to Faith's melodic voice.

This time when he woke it wasn't to thunder, or a terrified horse, it was to Faith's voice.

"Gabriel. Go get into bed.

Gabriel's eyes fluttered open to see Faith kneeling in front of him. "The horse?"

"She's fast asleep. The storm is over," Faith assured him.

Gabriel felt his heart swell with love for this woman he hardly knew. Every time he learned something more about her, he fell a little deeper in love with her. "You were wunderbaar..."

Faith smiled tiredly. "So was Peony. She kept me calm."

Gabriel knew it had been the other way around, but he was too focused on Faith's face to even argue. He reached out, as if he was still in a dream, and framed her face. "I never expected you..."

Faith's smile was slow as she let out a quiet sigh. "I didn't expect you either."

Neither of them said a word, but the moment was so laden with unsaid words that Gabriel could feel the air crackling with more than just the aftermath of a storm.

He felt it crackle with anticipation.

Faith suddenly drew back and stood up. "I'm going to… start breakfast."

Before Gabriel could apologize for his honesty, Faith rushed out of the barn, leaving nothing but her scent to haunt Gabriel until he saw her again.

# Chapter 13
# Doubt Circles the Mind

Two weeks after the storm that ravaged through Lancaster County, it was with hesitance that Faith wrote another letter to Isaac. Ever since she had written to explain about her need to stay in Lancaster for another month, his letters to her seemed a little strange.

Faith couldn't say it was one thing in particular, but it felt as if his letters were disconnected and almost forced. When she mentioned about the horses being frightened of the storm and how she had helped Gabriel calm them down, Isaac had clarified that if it had been him, she would've been sent back to the house.

According to Isaac, women had no business interrupting a man, and no place in a barn.

Faith found it odd that his words were so harsh and couldn't understand why she dreaded Isaac's letters instead of looking forward to them. She tried her best to remember what about Isaac had attracted her to him in the first place, but the more she tried, the more she wondered if they had ever really connected at all.

Like she had connected with Gabriel.

Guilt had appeared permanently in her life, taunting her about her ever-growing emotions for Gabriel. She couldn't remember feeling this way about Isaac and couldn't help but fear that when she returned to Ohio, her feelings for Gabriel would overshadow her courtship with Isaac.

It was wrong. Faith knew it.

But she also didn't know how to remedy the situation.

The two men were vastly different in every way that mattered. Not only were their appearances completely opposites from each other, their personalities were as well. Whereas Isaac was very opinionated and had firm beliefs about a woman's place in his life, Gabriel was kind and had a way of making her feel appreciated.

When she had packed a picnic basket for a buggy ride with Isaac, he had complained about the sandwich filling and the chocolate cookies, because he preferred ginger. The one time she had packed Gabriel lunch to the field, he hadn't complained once and instead had been grateful for her efforts.

Just like conflicting feelings with the men in her life, Faith felt conflicted about the different communities. Something about Lancaster County appealed to her, even though she had always loved Ohio. She had yet to decide about what she was going to do with her heritage, but for now, she only knew that she loved and appreciate her grandfather's farm.

She knew that keeping it would only cause complications, but Faith doubted whether she could sell it. Although she knew Gabriel loved the farm and would care for it, it felt wrong to profit from her grandfather's death.

She'd rather keep her half of the farm and...

And that's where her trail of thought stopped every time.

She couldn't move to Lancaster County.

She had Isaac, and her family, and her friends in Ohio. All she had in Lancaster County was a man that confused, intrigued, and fascinated her; and a farm that she did not know what she was going to do with.

Half a farm, that is.

She glanced at the empty page before her and wondered what she was going to write to Isaac. Whenever she told him about the farm, his reply was the same: she shouldn't interfere with Gabriel's work. If she told him how beautiful Lancaster County was, he pointed out that it wasn't her home. It felt as if she couldn't say anything to him without being corrected, chastened, or ignored.

A heavy sigh escaped her as her hand hovered over the writing pad. Before she wrote, she prayed that this time Isaac's response would be better. That he would at least try to understand her, listen to her, and tell her he missed her.

*My dearest Isaac*

*Since we last spoke, I hope you are doing well. I am becoming homesick for our farm, our community, and our small town.*

*I miss the fields that stretch as far as the eye can see. I miss my mamm's cooking and I miss our buggy rides. I miss how we talked and dreamed of the future. Although I appreciate your letters, I find it different from talking to you in person.*

*I can't help but wish that things might have been different. I'm grateful that my grosspappi had the heart to leave something to me in his will, but it's hard for me to be away from home.*

*When the thirty days are over, I will be able to sell my half of the farm to Gabriel and yet I'm not sure that is what I want to do. Would my grosspappi have wanted me to sell my heritage, my mamm's childhood home?*

*These are the questions I struggle with while I am here.*

*Then I try to think of the future and what wunderbaar blessings await us.*

*Have you been busy? I hope you haven't forgotten about me altogether? One of these days I'll be home and we can go on a picnic again. This time I'll remember that you don't like cucumbers and pack ginger cookies instead of chocolate.*

*My sincerest regards,*
*Faith*

Faith read the letter over and hoped that it would reconnect her with Isaac in the way it had connected them before she had come to Lancaster County. But even as she sealed the envelope, she wondered if she wanted to continue with Isaac.

Although he was her sweetheart, she was struggling when she thought of a future with him.

Gabriel wasn't the reason for that, but deep-down Faith knew he was part of it.

# Chapter 14
# Dreams of the Future

Gabriel no longer checked the mailbox. He couldn't help but feel his hopes crush and his heart break every time he saw a letter from Ohio. Although he knew Faith received letters from both her mother and her sweetheart, he had quickly come to distinguish between the two handwritings.

A letter that was in the mailbox this morning was from him.

Gabriel was going to be left on his own by the man that would take Faith back to Ohio. What had been his dream when Faith had arrived had now become something he dreaded.

He hadn't touched the letter, instead he had left it in the mailbox for Faith to find. He knew she checked every morning.

Instead, Gabriel had tended to the farm and spent his day in the field. There was much work to be done and the more work he did, the more he hoped that time would pass by quicker. There were only twelve days left between now and the day that Faith had to decide what she was going to do with her part of the inheritance.

Gabriel had wanted her to sell her share to him, now he wanted her to stay.

But he knew that was a dream of a foolish man. A man that needed to accept that Faith's heart was already taken. By the time lunchtime rolled around, he was hesitant to go in. He couldn't see Faith smiling with excitement after having received another letter from her sweetheart.

That night in the barn, during the storm, Gabriel had fallen even deeper. The morning after when she had woken him, he had realized that his heart now belonged to her, although he knew she might not feel the same way.

But surely, she had to at least feel the connection between them?

It wasn't Gabriel's place to ask; it wasn't his place to hope, and it surely wasn't his place to feel angry and envious every time she received a letter from her sweetheart.

After washing his hands by the water pump, he made his way around to the large back porch. He stopped just short when he noticed Faith sitting in a rocking chair, clearly terribly upset.

"Faith?" Gabriel asked, rushing up the stairs. "Did you get hurt? Was there another snake?"

She wasn't his to care for, but Gabriel couldn't help but want to make the tears disappear from her face.

She shook her head and sniffed. "I'm not hurt and there wasn't a snake, but there was this," Faith said, holding up the letter Gabriel had seen in the mailbox.

"A letter from your... Isaac?" he couldn't let the words sweetheart cross his lips when he saw the devastation in her eyes.

"Apparently he's not *my* Isaac anymore." Faith laughed wryly before another tear slipped down her cheek.

"What happened?" Gabriel asked, feeling anger rush through his veins, knowing that Isaac had upset her.

"I'm not sure, really. It seems I inherited half a farm from a grandfather I didn't know, came to Lancaster County, agreed to stay to meet the terms of the will for both your sake and mine…. While Isaac decided that patience wasn't one of his strongest suits."

Gabriel waited for her to continue, not sure how he should respond.

"From what I understand, Isaac has concluded that we're not suited. He's been spending some time with his friend and fell in love with Sarah Bontrager, his friend's schweschder. Apparently, Sarah is kind and knows her place, and she's now his new sweetheart," Faith finished with a heavy sigh.

"He sent you a letter to break up with you?" Gabriel asked, horrified.

"Jah, apparently the thought of waiting until I returned was simply too much to ask," Faith sniffed.

"That's poor taste, not gentlemanly at all. I hope you tell him that," Gabriel said, feeling even angrier at the man he'd never met.

"Nee, I won't humiliate myself by writing to him again. I thought… I thought his letters seemed strange, but I wasn't sure why. At least now I know." Faith wiped her eyes and drew in a deep breath. "So that's that then."

Gabriel wanted to wrap his arms around her to console her, but he knew it would be inappropriate. He hated seeing Faith this upset, but deep down, he couldn't help but feel relieved. Now that Faith was free of her relationship with Isaac, he could start working on a relationship of his own.

"Levi always quoted the bible when things happened we couldn't explain or didn't expect." Gabriel sat down beside Faith and glanced out over the fields. *The Lord has made everything for its purpose. Proverbs 16:4.* You might not understand why this happened now, but one day you will look back at today and understand exactly why it had to happen to you."

Faith turned to him, a smile softly curving the corners of her mouth. "That's a beautiful verse Gabriel, I'll find peace in it knowing that the Lord has orchestrated this, just as he orchestrated me coming to Lancaster County. I just hope that you're right. That one day there comes a time that I understand why."

"That time will come, but for today... why don't I make us lunch?" Gabriel asked with a cheerful smile.

"Ach nee, I don't expect you to busy yourself in the kitchen after working in the fields all morning," Faith said, standing up.

Gabriel shook his head and stood up. "You take a seat, I offered. It might not be as delicious as your lunches, but at least it will be food."

Faith's soft laughter followed him into the kitchen. Gabriel wouldn't tell her now, but the tears she had just spilled had lined the way for him to make his own dreams of a future come true.

# Chapter 15
# Something More?

Faith had expected Isaac's news to be devastating, not to feel relieved merely days after having read it.

When she had gotten over the initial upset and feelings of betrayal that had led her to cry on the porch where Gabriel had found her, she actually felt as if someone had lifted a burden from her shoulders.

That night she had lain in bed and thought of Gabriel's words. Everything in life happened for a purpose, Gott's purpose.

That didn't mean that she didn't still feel slightly upset with Isaac, but it meant that she didn't question the why's and whatnots of his letter. She hadn't written back, although she had received a letter from her mother the following day, stating that she wasn't sure how to tell Faith of Isaac's betrayal.

It was still hard for Faith to believe that Isaac had simply moved on the moment she was out of sight. She felt somewhat betrayed, but as the days passed, she felt the weight lifted from her shoulders. She no longer had an invisible string tugging her back to Ohio, or commitments making her wish the time away.

Instead, she savored every day and, if she was honest, Gabriel's company too.

"Did you hear what I said?" Gabriel asked, smiling at her across the table.

Faith shook her head as she smiled at Gabriel. "I'm sorry. I didn't hear the last part. What did the man at the hardware store say?"

Gabriel had been entertaining her with a tale about a man that had come into the hardware store this morning while he had been there. Apparently, the man, a young Englischer, had been complaining about the cost of lamps.

"He told him he should stop complaining because at least they had electricity to run the bulbs."

Faith smiled. "And here we have been with no lamps or electricity for years."

"Exactly," Gabriel continued with a gleeful look in his eyes. "I couldn't stop myself. I know it was probably rude of me, but I stepped forward and said, 'I've never had electricity and never complained about it.'"

"Gabriel, you didn't?" Faith asked, mortified.

"I did. I've known John at the hardware store for years and, of course, he laughed, but the other man's eyes widened as if they were saucers before he muttered something about having to be somewhere and running out of the store."

Faith and Gabriel laughed. Faith could only imagine how bad the man must've felt knowing an Amish person had heard the entire conversation. "You're horrible."

"I know," Gabriel agreed easily.

Their laugher faded and silence hung over the table. Faith glanced up and met Gabriel's gaze, feeling her heart swell with affection. She looked forward to their shared meals. He always had a story to delight her with, or something interesting about the farm she enjoyed learning about. He never treated her as if it wasn't her place to ask a question or to have an opinion.

Instead, Faith fell a little more for him with every passing day. She only had one week left in Lancaster County and for the first time since leaving Ohio on a bus, Faith could suddenly not imagine going back.

"Have you decided?" Gabriel asked, as if reading her mind.

Faith shrugged with a shake of head. "Nee, but I mean, what choice could there really be? I can't stay here, can I?"

Gabriel's mouth opened, but he closed it again before he stood up from the table. "I'm going to head to bed."

"Good night," Faith said to his back as he quickly left the kitchen.

She wasn't sure what he was about to say, but she could see that he had all but fled.

The decision she had to make in a week weighed heavily on her mind. The more she thought about it, the more Faith wondered why her grandfather had wanted her to come here. She could understand the inheritance, but why the conditions?

Was there something here he wanted her to see?

Or was there someone here he wanted her to meet?

The more Faith thought about it, the more she wondered if her grandfather hadn't bought her here to meet Gabriel?

From what she knew about her grandfather, both he and Gabriel had been very fond of each other. But her grandfather hadn't ever met her.

Why else would he have given them each half of his farm?

It wasn't as if Faith could farm her half and Gabriel his. To split up a property as majestic as her grandfather's would be sacrilege.

Faith gathered the plates and filled the sink full of soapy water. Only when bubbles spilled over the side onto her shoes did she realize she'd been watching the barn and thinking of Gabriel.

Suddenly, the thought of leaving Lancaster County didn't seem so impossible. It was the thought of leaving Gabriel.

Somehow, during the almost four weeks since her arrival, she appreciated having Gabriel in her life. Although Ohio had her family and her friends, Faith wasn't sure she would be able to forget Gabriel.

He had opened her eyes to a new life. He had introduced her to a part of the world she had never known, and more than anything, he had become a trusted friend. She had confided in him about her fears of leaving Ohio. He had consoled her after Isaac had broken up with her, and even now he encouraged her to make the best decision for her.

Not for him.

The only problem was, Faith did not know what that decision was.

If she sold her half of the farm to Gabriel, it would mean going back to Ohio and never seeing him again. If she kept her half, he would never forgive her for taking away his dream.

It didn't matter which way she decided, Gabriel was going to be angry.

When she finally climbed into bed that night, she dreamed of a third option. An option where she stayed in Lancaster County, keeping her half of the farm and spending the rest of her life with Gabriel on *their* farm.

Faith smiled in her sleep, because her dream was the best solution to the problem at hand.

Only it wasn't a choice she could make without knowing how Gabriel felt.

# Chapter 16
# Familye & Roots

Exactly thirty days after Gabriel's last appointment with the lawyer, he stopped the buggy in front of the lawyer's offices. A month ago, he couldn't wait to buy Faith's share of the farm, even if that meant getting a loan from the bank and paying it off for the rest of his life.

But today his heart was heavy.

With the required allotment of time now sufficiently served, Gabriel didn't want Faith to leave. Over the last month, he experienced feelings he had never expected to feel. He wanted to build a future with Faith instead of just wanting her to sell him her share of the farm.

As they walked into the lawyer's offices, he glanced at Faith. Her expression was neutral and no matter how hard he tried to guess, Gabriel wasn't sure what she was going to do. What if she changed her mind and wanted to stay in Lancaster County? Would that mean that he would need to give up half of the land he had farmed for such a long time? Who kept the house? Who would use the barn? There simply wasn't a fair way to split a farm in half.

The one thing Gabriel had dreamed of he couldn't imagine happening. Ever since Faith had received the letter from Isaac, Gabriel couldn't be sure whether she had any feelings for him at all. He was so certain of her affections that he wanted to drop on his knee and ask her for her hand in marriage, right there and then. And then other times...

Other times, he could see her mind drift off to a place he didn't recognize. He couldn't help but wonder if she dreamed of going back to Ohio in those times. If she was counting the days until she could say goodbye to Gabriel and her grandfather's notions of forcing her to get to know her roots?

It was a strange feeling for Gabriel, who had always known who he was and where he wanted to be.

"Are you ready?" Faith asked him as they took a seat in the waiting area.

"Jah," Gabriel nodded, feeling a little more than anxious of what was about to happen.

The lawyer had only sent a message the day before that they were to come and see him. Perhaps there were more additions to the will he hadn't known about. Perhaps neither of them could sell and they had no choice but to keep the farm together or to sell it together.

When the lawyer's office door opened and he invited them inside, Gabriel drew in a deep breath and turned to Faith with a nervous smile. "Whatever happens in there, I want you to know that I'll always be grateful for meeting you and for spending this time with you. Meeting you has... it changed it me," Gabriel admitted quietly.

It was the closest he had ever come to telling her how he felt. But now wasn't the time for emotional admissions. It was time to find out what the future held for them.

For both of them.

Mr. Anderson was waiting for them with a welcoming smile. "Gabriel, Faith, welcome. This is the first time I see the two of you at once. How have you been?"

Faith sat down and smiled. "Very gut, denke."

"The same," Gabriel agreed.

"Since you've both been well, I won't keep you in suspense for another moment. The day I gave Gabriel the letters your grandfather had written to you, I received one of my own. One to explain why he had stated these conditions in his will. One he wanted me to read to you after we had completed the thirty days," Mr. Anderson explained, opening an envelope similar to the ones Gabriel and Faith had received.

"Right, it starts with the terms of his will, stating that you have to live together on the property for thirty days before either of you could sell your inheritance. Then here... this is what he wanted me to read to you." Mr. Anderson cleared his throat before he read.

*A man doesn't reach my age without learning some important lessons in life. Lessons that one doesn't simply learn in a school book, lessons that you have to experience to understand their truth.*

*I always believed that familye was the blessings Gott bestowed on me through my parents, grandparents, aunts, uncles, cousins... you understand. But it took taking Gabriel in to learn that familye isn't always blood.*

*Sometimes it's a little boy in a care home, needing a familye. Someone to care for them, to love and teach them, someone to always be there for them. Gabriel, you might not* be my seeh, but I have loved you like one for my entire life. I know you don't have any familye of your own, but after living with Faith for the last month, I hope you appreciate how important familye can be.

Familye we sometimes choose for ourselves, and when we do, we learn that no argument, harsh word, or impatient comment can't be forgiven. We learn to laugh together, to mourn together and, most of all, to build together. Although you and Faith only shared a short amount of time together in the greater span of things, I hope that you finally understand why I always encouraged you to find someone to share your life with.

No man is a lone wolf, my dearest Gabriel. We all need someone and it's time you found yours.

Faith, the reason I asked you to stay is completely different. You were born and raised in Ohio and although I'm certain your mamm often spoke of her familye and life in Lancaster County, you only appreciated the roots you experienced for yourself.

Back home, you probably have a favorite spot in the yard, a favorite place where you go to be alone, and you have all the friends and familye you've known your whole life. Those are the roots of your daed's familye. I was selfish in my will, wanting you to come to Lancaster County to experience your mamm's roots as well. She had a different life before Ohio. I wanted you to see the farm that our familye has farmed for generations, and most of all I wanted you to have something to remember me by.

It might not be memories of spending time with me in the fields, but at least you'll always have this last month to *remind you of the grandfather you never met and the familye heritage you never understood.*

*Our roots and our familye make us the people we are. I don't doubt that you were both upset to learn about the terms of my will, but I hope that you now understand why I did it. Gabriel, you learned the importance of familye and Faith, you learned about your roots.*

*Now that this old man has made a point, even in death, you are free to do with the property as you choose. Any decision you make will have my blessing, as long as it's a decision you can live with.*

*Levi Stoltzfus.*

Mr. Anderson folded the letter and took off his glasses before turning first to Gabriel and then to Faith. "So, what would you like to do?"

# Chapter 17
# A Buggy Ride

Faith couldn't help but feel a little emotional after listening to the lawyer reading the letter. Suddenly, she understood why it was so important for her grandfather to want her to come to Lancaster County. That, along with Gabriel's words right before they walked in, made her confused and more than a little doubtful of the decision she wanted to make.

She looked up and found both the lawyer and Gabriel waiting for her answer. "I uh..." she said, turning to Gabriel with a wide-eyed expression.

There was so much she wanted to say to Gabriel. She wanted to tell him how much he meant to her and how much she enjoyed the last month as well, but the lawyer was sitting right there.

Waiting for her.

Waiting for her decision.

A decision that would alienate Gabriel from her if not explained.

"Faith? It seems that Gabriel is leaving the decision in your hands. Have you decided? I'm sure you're eager to return home?" the lawyer asked gently.

Faith glanced at Gabriel, trying to explain to him what she was about to do, but from his guarded expression it was clear he wouldn't understand.

"I'm keeping my half," Faith said simply, not knowing how else to articulate her decision.

Gabriel's eyes darkened with disappointment and surprise. "You're keeping it?"

"Jah," Faith nodded.

"Then I guess unless Gabriel wants to sell, there's nothing more to be said," Mr. Anderson said, glancing at Gabriel with a questioning look.

Gabriel shook his head and stood up. "I'm not selling my half either." His words were hard and cold, as if making it clear that Faith had no right to take his dream from him.

Before she could even try to explain, Gabriel walked out the door, leaving her and the lawyer alone.

"I have to go," Faith said apologetically before she rushed after him. He was already sitting in the buggy, his gaze distant and his eyes cold.

Faith climbed in and before she could even attempt to tell him why she had made that decision, he took the reins and called to the horse to move. Her temper rose, hating that he treated her like a stranger. She knew he didn't understand and as they drove out of town, she knew she wouldn't wait to explain. She leaned over and reached for the reins.

Gabriel turned to her with a surprised expression when she pulled on them and called *a halt* to the horse. The horse obeyed without complaint, but Gabriel was a matter of a whole different kind.

"I'm driving," Gabriel snapped at her, trying to take the reins back.

"And I have something to say," Faith snapped right back, still holding fast to the reins.

"Then make it fast. I have *half* a farm to tend to," Gabriel said through clenched teeth.

Faith narrowed her gaze and tried to see behind the anger and the disappointment. "Did you mean what you said before we went in?"

His eyes softened marginally. "That you changed me? Jah, you did. Satisfied? Apparently, that's what Levi had hoped for all along."

Faith nodded, a smile curving her mouth. "You changed me as well, Gabriel. This last month... It was more than I could've ever imagined. This morning when we stopped in front of the lawyer's office, I was certain that it was time to go back to Ohio, but then... Then I saw in your eyes what I feel in my heart."

Gabriel's eyes widened with surprise. "What do you mean?"

Faith shook her head. "If you want my honesty, I need yours first."

Gabriel paused, as if considering whether he could trust her with his heart before he spoke. "I was happy when Isaac broke things off with you. I know I'm a terrible person for it, but I wanted you to be available."

"Why?" Faith asked with a cute frown.

"Because I hoped to court you myself," Gabriel admitted with a sigh. "I know it's foolish, but there you have it."

Faith laughed. "It's not foolish, Gabriel, because I feel the same way. I didn't at first, but the thought of leaving Lancaster County, leaving you... I can't imagine leaving here and never seeing you again."

"So you kept the farm to come and check on me?" Gabriel asked, confused.

Faith smiled at him and rested her hand on his cheek. "Nee, I kept my half because I hoped... I hoped that maybe someday we could farm it together. That we could build a future here together."

Gabriel's eyes lit up with hope, his smile reaching from ear to ear. "You want to stay. You're not just keeping your half to spite me; you're keeping it to build a future with me?"

Faith nodded. "Roots and familye."

Gabriel reached for her hand and gently pressed a kiss on top of it. "In that case, Faith Glick, might I be so bold as to ask you to go on a buggy ride with me?"

Faith's laughter carried on the wind. "I'd love to go on a buggy ride with you, Gabriel. Especially if it's the first of many."

# Epilogue

Faith carefully laid the flowers on the grave before she stood back. She drew in a deep breath, filling her lungs with fresh air before she turned to her husband. "I wish I could've met him."

Gabriel rested an arm over her shoulders and pressed a kiss to her prayer kapp. "In a way, you did."

"I did, didn't I?" Faith laughed as they walked through the fields back towards the farm.

"I have to admit, I never thought Levi could be so connivingly clever. Do you think he knew that we'd fall in love?" Gabriel asked.

Faith smiled with a shrug. "I don't think he knew, but I think he hoped. Why else insist I spend a month on the farm, knowing you'd have to sleep in the hayloft?"

"It was touch and go there for a while. Especially with you all but living at the mailbox while waiting for Isaac's next letter," Gabriel teased.

Faith playfully punched her husband. "I didn't live at the mailbox; I simply kept an eye out. And now, looking back, I think I was so eager to hear from Isaac because I hoped every time that his next letter would make me feel the way I did when I was with you."

"So you've forgiven him?" Gabriel cocked a brow.

"There was nothing to forgive. I still think he could've waited for me to come back before courting another girl, but like Levi said, everything happens for a reason. Even Isaac courting someone else happened for a reason."

"And you keeping your half of the farm..." Gabriel teased.

"I still remember how surprised my parents were when I told them I was coming right back to Lancaster County after packing my things." Faith shook her head.

She had returned home a few days after meeting with the lawyer, with Gabriel by her side. After introducing him to her familye she had told her parents of her decision only to be gawked at as if she had grown two heads.

But in the two weeks that followed, her mother came to understand how much she and Gabriel cared for each other. Gabriel had asked for her father's blessing and before Faith knew it, she was married by her own bishop and headed back to Lancaster County, a married woman.

"Do you ever think we got married too soon?" Gabriel asked thoughtfully as they approached the house.

Faith thought for a moment before she smiled and shook her head. "Gabriel, if there is one thing I learned over this last year, is that if something feels right, it's right. From the moment I told you I was keeping the farm right until now, I've never had a single regret. You're the mann Gott chose for me long before I even considered courting. This farm is the home I never knew, and this life is the one that had been waiting for me all along."

Gabriel grinned. "So then you're happy."

Faith laughed. "I'm overjoyed. And you?"

Gabriel shrugged. "I'm happy. I'll be overjoyed if you cook us stew for dinner. The way only you can."

Faith cocked a brow. "What if I told you I want to rest for a while instead?"

Gabriel frowned and stepped in front of her. "Is something wrong?" Concern laced his voice even as he searched her gaze.

Faith shook her head. "Nothing that won't be remedied in nine months."

Gabriel looked confused for a moment before his eyes widened with surprise. "You're with child?"

Faith laughed as she felt her heart spill over with love and joy. "I am. I went to see the Englisch doctor yesterday. We're having a boppli. He said the fatigue, nausea, and headaches are normal in the first three months."

Gabriel lifted her onto her feet and swung her in a wide circle before putting her down, a big smile on his face. "Then you need to rest. Building a boppli is hard work, I've heard."

Faith shook her head. "I'm not building a baby, I'm growing one."

"It's the same thing. Except, you're growing our roots, our future, and our familye." Gabriel's eyes softened as he stepped closer and took Faith's hand in his.

A tear slipped over her cheek; her cup overflowed.

When she had learned of her grandfather in Lancaster County, Faith had thought it would be a quick trip to deal with her inheritance before she returned home. But now, as she looked into her husband's loving gaze, standing on the ground that generations of her familye had farmed before her, she knew that this was where she belonged.

Between the hills was where she belonged. The horses were calm on storm nights in the barn.

But most of all, she belonged with Gabriel.

What she had considered a foolish old man's demands had turned out to be the makings of her and Gabriel's love story. A love story she knew she would cherish for the rest of her life. And one day, she would take her daughter on a walk to the creek and tell her how to know the difference between liking someone and finding your soulmate.

Because if Faith hadn't learned the difference, her life would've looked a lot different now.

She smiled at Gabriel and knew that her life was exactly how it was meant to be.

*** The End ***


Thank you kindly for choosing to read my book. I sincerely hope you enjoyed it. All of my Amish Romances are wholesome stories suitable for all to enjoy.